Mrs. Jeepers' Monster Class Trip

There are more books about the Bailey School Kids!
Have you read these adventures?

Mrs. Jeepers' Monster Class Trip

by Debbie Dadey
and
Marcia Thornton Jones

illustrated by John Steven Gurney

A
LITTLE APPLE
PAPERBACK

SCHOLASTIC INC.
New York Toronto London Auckland Sydney
Mexico City New Delhi Hong Kong

No part of this work may be reproduced, stored in a retrieval system, or transmitted in any form or by any means, electronic, mechanical, photocopying, recording, or otherwise, without written permission of the publisher. For information regarding permission, write to Scholastic Inc., Attention: Permissions Department, 555 Broadway, New York, NY 10012.

ISBN 0-439-21585-4

Text copyright © 2000 by Marcia Thornton Jones and Debra S. Dadey.
Illustrations copyright © 2000 by Scholastic Inc.
All rights reserved. Published by Scholastic Inc.
SCHOLASTIC, LITTLE APPLE PAPERBACKS,
THE ADVENTURES OF THE BAILEY SCHOOL KIDS, and associated logos are trademarks and/or registered trademarks of Scholastic Inc.

12 11 10 9   3 4 5/0

Printed in the U.S.A.
First Scholastic printing, September 2000

For Jordan, Dina, Linda,
and Paul Jurgaitis — DD

For Paul Brett Johnson — thanks
for helping me chisel words into stories
— MTJ

Contents

Contents

1

Stone of Destiny

"Look what I have!" Howie yelled to Liza, Melody, and Eddie. It was Thursday morning, right before the school bell. His friends waited for him under the big oak tree on the playground. Howie pulled a small green book out of his backpack to show his friends.

"What's so great about a book?" Eddie complained.

"This isn't just any book," Howie said. "This is the best rock book in the world. It's fascinating."

Eddie grunted and turned his baseball cap around backward. The only things that interested him were sports or monsters. Howie's book, *The Complete Field Guide to Rocks, Gems, and Minerals*, had neither one. "Rocks are only good when you can shoot them in a slingshot," Eddie pointed out.

Liza shook her head. "You could put your eye out with a slingshot."

Melody took the book from Howie. "This is the perfect book for our class trip this weekend."

"Class trip?" Eddie asked.

Liza rolled her eyes and pushed blond bangs out of her face. "Don't you remember our class is going to Rock Castle State Park tomorrow? We'll be gone the entire weekend. We even get to miss school on Friday and Monday!"

"Awesome!" Eddie strummed his fingers on a pretend guitar. "Is that a big castle where they play rock music?"

Melody laughed. "Not exactly. Weren't you listening when Mrs. Jeepers told us about the rocks and gems they have at Rock Castle on the other side of Sheldon City?"

Eddie shrugged his shoulders. He must

have been daydreaming when their teacher talked about it. "Why would anyone want to make a castle full of rocks? It seems like a waste to me."

"Rocks are cool," Howie said. "There are so many different kinds. Some are very valuable. There's one crystal called painite that is priceless because there are only three known pieces of painite in existence — and nobody knows where they are."

"That's because they're hidden in that silly book," Eddie teased.

Melody turned the pages of Howie's book. She pointed to a picture of a beautiful blue stone with a star shining in the middle. "It says here that some rocks and gems are thought to have mysterious powers. This star sapphire is called the Stone of Destiny."

"That's a bunch of baloney. How can a rock have powers?" Eddie asked.

Liza caught a yellow leaf as it fell off

3

the oak tree. She twirled the leaf in her hands. "Have you forgotten about Mrs. Jeepers' brooch?" she asked.

They all stared at the leaf and thought about their teacher, Mrs. Jeepers. Some of the kids in their third-grade class believed she was a vampire. After all, she lived in a haunted house, came from Transylvania, and wore a mysterious brooch that seemed to have magical powers. Whenever anyone in Bailey Elementary was mischievous, Mrs. Jeepers would rub the green stone in her brooch. As if by magic, everyone would stop misbehaving.

"I read that there's one diamond that brings bad luck to anyone who owns it," Howie said, trying not to think about Mrs. Jeepers. "It's called the Hope Diamond."

Eddie slapped his forehead. "I must have the Hope Diamond in my pocket," he complained. "That's why I'm unlucky enough to have to go on this dumb class trip to look at rocks."

"I agree with Eddie," Liza said with a gulp. "I don't want to go anywhere that has rocks with mysterious powers." She threw her leaf down and looked ready to cry.

"Don't be a wimp," Eddie said. "We won't be that lucky. The only rocks they'll have at Rock Castle are plain, boring gray ones. If we have to drive all the way to Sheldon City, I wish we could go someplace exciting, like the Sheldon City Racetrack."

Howie patted Liza on the shoulder. "Don't worry. We'll have fun at Rock Castle. We're going to camp out and my mom said there's swimming and hiking in the park."

"I guess anything is better than doing math homework," Eddie grumbled.

"There's nothing to worry about," Melody said. "After all, it's not like rocks can come to life."

2

Rock Castle

"I think we made a wrong turn and ended up on Mars," Eddie said, looking out the bus window. It was Friday morning and the bus was loaded with Bailey City third-graders on their way to Rock Castle State Park for their weekend class trip.

"It's creepy looking," Liza said from the seat behind Eddie and Howie.

Melody whispered from beside Liza, "Everything looks dead."

All the kids on the bus had been singing and talking, but now they got quiet and stared outside. In Bailey City the grass had been green and the trees were shades of red and yellow, but now rolling lumps of gray and black rock covered the ground as far as they could see.

7

Every once in a while a scraggly plant blew in the wind, struggling to survive.

Their teacher, Mrs. Jeepers, cleared her throat and spoke from the front of the bus. "This area is covered with rock formed from the lava of an ancient volcano."

"Holy Toledo!" Eddie yelled and hopped up from his seat. "Are we going to see oozing red-hot lava?"

Liza turned pale and grabbed Melody's arm. "Oh my gosh, we could get hurt if the volcano erupts while we're here."

"The volcano in this area is extinct," Mrs. Jeepers explained. "It will probably never erupt again."

"Too bad," Eddie said. "I wanted to see some action."

Mrs. Jeepers flashed her eyes at Eddie and gently rubbed the green brooch at her throat. Eddie quickly sat down beside Howie.

"Lava is hot liquid rock called magma that has escaped to the earth's surface," Mrs. Jeepers explained. "Once this entire area was covered with lava. When lava cools, it becomes rock. Igneous rock. That is what you see outside the windows."

The bus went over a big bump and Eddie waved his hand in the air. "Will we at least get to see a real volcano?" he asked.

Mrs. Jeepers smiled her odd little half smile and pointed out the window to distant rocky cliffs jutting up to the sky. "No, we will not be seeing the extinct volcano during this trip. We're going to Rock Castle State Park to learn about sedimentary rocks formed by ancient oceans."

Eddie slumped down into his seat. "Rats," he said. "At least an exploding volcano would be interesting."

"A little too interesting," Liza said, relieved that they weren't going to be showered with hot lava.

The bus continued toward the cliffs. Soon the gray and black rocks disappeared. Now the ground was covered by sandy soil and ragged cliffs outlined the sky.

"We are nearing the park," Mrs. Jeepers told the students. "We can already see many fascinating rock formations."

"Rocks are boring," Eddie complained and pulled his baseball cap down over his eyes.

Howie pointed out the window. "Not that rock. It looks just like a shark."

Eddie peered out the dirty window. Huge rocks jutted up toward the sky. Some stood taller than the bus, casting eerie shadows over the kids inside.

Liza giggled nervously. "That fat one looks like a duck."

"The one next to it looks like an elephant," Melody said.

"There are some crazy-looking rocks," Eddie agreed. "The ones on top of the cliff look like an entire squadron of vampires getting ready to ambush the bus."

Liza looked ready to faint. "What if they really are vampire monsters?" she asked Melody.

Melody patted Liza on the back. "Don't worry," Melody told her friend. "They're only rocks."

Liza sighed and was glad when the bus finally pulled to a stop beside a big stone sign that read ROCK CASTLE LODGE. But

she wasn't very happy when she saw where they were going to spend the night. Chiseled into the side of a soaring cliff, Rock Castle Lodge looked more like a haunted mansion than a place to learn about rocks.

"My dad told me this place is over a hundred years old," Melody said. "It was built by a crazy old lady who loved rocks so much she built her house out of them."

"Cool," Eddie said as the kids hopped off the bus. They all carried backpacks and duffel bags loaded with sleeping bags, flashlights, and other camping gear. "This place might not be so boring after all. Check out that neat tower."

A dark tower rose high over the rest of the mansion. The tower was made of stones and looked like a turret on a castle. Liza shivered when she thought she saw a figure staring down from the windows. She forgot all about the tower when the huge wooden door to Rock Castle Lodge squeaked open.

A tall, gray figure floated out the door. "Oh no," Liza squealed. "It's a monster!"

3

Secrets of Life

"Liza's right," Eddie said. "That lady looks older than dirt. Maybe she's a mud monster."

"SHHH," Melody hissed. "You'll hurt her feelings."

Liza's face turned red as the gray-haired woman smiled at the group of third-graders. "Welcome to Rock Castle. I am Mrs. Granite, the geologist," she said. "Please follow me inside."

"What's a geologist?" Eddie asked. "Is that someone who cures strange diseases?"

Howie shook his head. Howie knew about the different kinds of scientists. After all, his father was a scientist at the Federal Aeronautics Technology Station, or F.A.T.S. for short. "A geologist studies

ROCK CASTLE
LODGE

the earth's rocks and minerals," Howie explained.

Huge stone walls surrounded the kids as they entered Rock Castle. The stone ceiling was so high Eddie figured it would echo like a canyon. "Hello," Eddie yelled to try it out. Sure enough, his voice bounced around the large room. "HELLO, HELLO."

Mrs. Jeepers frowned at Eddie and touched her brooch. Eddie quickly closed his mouth and pulled off his base-ball cap. He pretended to be interested in the mud caked on his sneakers.

"This looks like Rock City, USA," Melody said softly, careful not to make an echo. She had never seen so many rocks in one place. The walls of the large room were lined with displays and there were hundreds of glass-topped tables filled with different types of rocks. Mrs. Granite started telling the group about the displays.

Eddie groaned at the thought of having

to study so many rocks. He looked around for something more interesting. At the far end of the huge room there was another door. Before anyone noticed, Eddie slipped over and turned the doorknob.

"Rats," Eddie said. "It's locked up tighter than my birthday presents."

A cold gray hand grabbed Eddie's shoulder. "Please stay with your group," Mrs. Granite told him. "It could save your life someday."

Eddie gulped as he stared into Mrs. Granite's gray eyes. "I was just curious to know what's behind that door," Eddie squeaked.

"It's only a storage room," Mrs. Granite said, pulling Eddie back to the other kids. "This weekend," Mrs. Granite continued, "you will learn about different types of rocks and gems. We will get to go on a learning hike and a fossil hunt. I even have a surprise for you at the end of our time together."

"I wonder what the surprise could be?" Liza whispered.

"She'll probably give us rock candy that's real rocks," Eddie grumbled.

"Now, let's take a look over here." Mrs. Granite gestured toward a huge wall of stones. "There are three types of rock," she explained. "Does anyone know what they are?"

Howie raised his hand and Mrs. Granite nodded to him. "Igneous, metamorphic, and sedimentary," he said proudly.

Mrs. Jeepers smiled at Howie and Mrs. Granite patted him on the back. "Excellent," Mrs. Granite told him.

"I don't understand," Eddie said.

Mrs. Granite repeated the three types of rock to Eddie. "No," Eddie said. "I don't understand why anyone cares about rocks. They're just lumps."

Mrs. Jeepers touched her hand to her brooch, but Mrs. Granite tapped her chin. "You're right," Mrs. Granite agreed. "Rocks are not always impressive in their natural state, but when they're polished you can see their inner beauty. Take these for instance." Mrs. Granite waved her gray-sleeved arm toward the display on the opposite wall.

"Wow!" Liza squealed as all the kids gasped at the new display. "These are beautiful."

Melody stared at the huge wall of polished gems. The gems were even prettier

than her mom's jewelry. In the middle of the display sat a bright green stone. It looked exactly like the stone in their teacher's brooch.

"These are quite breathtaking," Mrs. Granite said. "Some gems are even thought to have magical powers." She looked at Mrs. Jeepers, then at Eddie. "Perhaps you have heard of the famous French emperor Napoleon Bonaparte. He carried a sword with a diamond in it to bring him luck in battle."

"Cool," Eddie said. "Did it work?"

"Only for a while," Mrs. Granite said. "And England's Queen Elizabeth the First believed people could see visions in crystals."

"Do you believe that?" Liza asked.

"Not really," Mrs. Granite admitted. "But I do believe rocks hold the secrets of life."

"Perhaps they do," Mrs. Jeepers agreed.

Liza noticed that Mrs. Jeepers was

gently rubbing the green brooch at her neck. Liza wasn't the only one watching Mrs. Jeepers.

Mrs. Granite stared at Mrs. Jeepers' brooch as if it were a piece of candy Mrs. Granite just had to have.

4

Monster Garden

That night, Liza tossed and turned in her sleeping bag outside Rock Castle. Every time she moved, she felt another rock beneath her. A full moon rose high in the sky and cast odd shadows on the walls of the tent she shared with Melody and two other girls from her class. Liza flopped over again.

"Will you stop all that jumping around?" Melody mumbled from beside her. "I'm trying to sleep."

Liza propped herself up on her elbows and leaned over to Melody. "I have to tell you something," Liza whispered. "But I can't let anybody else hear."

Melody sighed and threw back her sleeping bag. Then she followed Liza out of the small tent. The moon gave them plenty of light so they could see Rock Castle looming high above them. Not a single light showed in any of the windows. "I don't know why we couldn't have slept inside the castle," Melody complained softly. "A castle ought to have plenty of beds."

"Maybe," Liza said softly, "there are things locked in all those rooms that Mrs. Granite doesn't want us to see."

A wolf howled in the distance, causing both girls to jump. "What is it you wanted to tell me?" Melody said with a gulp.

"Eddie and Howie need to hear this, too," Liza said. The girls sneaked around the girls' tents, being extra quiet as they passed Mrs. Jeepers' black tent. Eddie and Howie's tent was next to their teacher's. Liza stopped outside the boys' tent and softly tapped on the canvas.

Eddie stuck his head out the flap, but as soon as he saw Melody and Liza he opened the tent flap wide. Howie and Eddie stood there in their pajamas.

"What's up?" Eddie asked.

"We have a problem," Liza told them. "Follow me and I'll explain."

Liza pulled her friends into the shadows of Rock Castle. "I have a terrible feeling about this class trip."

Eddie nodded. "You're right. This trip is rotten because Mrs. Jeepers and Mrs. Granite are determined to make us learn about pebbles and stones. But they can't make me. I haven't learned a thing yet," Eddie said proudly.

Howie jabbed a finger in Eddie's chest. "You'd better start paying attention. You'll be in big trouble when Mrs. Jeepers gives us a test about rocks and you don't know any of the answers."

Liza shook her head. "I wish that learning about rocks was all we needed to worry about," she told him. "But if what I think is true, a science test is the least of our problems."

"I can't be in trouble," Eddie blurted out loud. "I haven't done anything bad. Yet."

"We'll all be in trouble if we don't keep our voices down," Melody warned and pointed to Mrs. Jeepers' tent. They waited to make sure their teacher wasn't going to jump out at them.

"I'm not talking about that kind of trouble," Liza said. "This afternoon I saw Mrs. Granite looking at Mrs. Jeepers' brooch," she explained. "I'm afraid that Mrs. Granite is going to steal Mrs. Jeepers' pin."

"That would be fine with me," Eddie said with a grin. "Then Mrs. Jeepers couldn't make me behave anymore."

"You'd still have to behave," Howie pointed out, "because deep down you're a nice kid and nice kids behave."

"Way, way down deep," Liza agreed.

Eddie puffed out his chest. "I don't have to do anything," he said, "unless I want to."

"You'd better want to be quiet, because I just heard something," Melody hissed.

27

"And whatever it is, it's coming this way!"

Heavy footsteps thudded on the gravel path and echoed around the tents. "It sounds like someone wearing lead boots," Eddie joked before Liza hushed him.

The kids pressed back into the shadows of Rock Castle and waited to see who was coming. It was Mrs. Granite. The tall geologist paused outside Mrs. Jeepers' tent. Mrs. Granite held her ear close to the tent door before a light came on inside the tent. Then she hurried back the way she had come, her heavy footsteps growing fainter as she walked away.

"Maybe Liza is right and Mrs. Granite does want to get her hands on Mrs. Jeepers' brooch," Howie whispered. "Why else would Mrs. Granite be hovering outside our teacher's tent?"

"Maybe she wanted to see if vampires

really sleep upside down," Eddie said matter-of-factly.

"I wonder where Mrs. Granite is going now?" Melody interrupted.

"There's one way to find out," Eddie told her. He didn't wait for his friends. He headed after Mrs. Granite.

Liza, Howie, and Melody looked at one another. Howie shrugged.

"We can't let him go alone," Howie said.

"Yes, we can," Melody pointed out.

"But we won't," Liza told her friends.

Melody sighed and Howie nodded. "Let's go," Liza said, and they hurried to catch up with Eddie.

The four friends followed Mrs. Granite around Rock Castle. They found themselves in a courtyard filled with marble statues. They weren't normal statues of people like in art museums. These were monster statues.

The kids quietly made their way

through the maze of giant art carved in stone. They passed statues of a two-headed dog, a monster with eight arms, and a giant three-tailed cat that looked ready to pounce.

"It looks like Mrs. Granite has a monster garden," Liza whispered with a shiver. The kids hid behind the cat statue as Mrs. Granite stopped in front of a statue of a woman whose head was covered with snakes. The geologist sat on a nearby bench and started talking in a low voice.

"Why would a geologist talk to a statue?" Melody asked.

"Maybe," Liza said slowly, "because she knows the statue can hear her!"

5

Life in Stone

Liza poked at the lumps in her oatmeal the next morning. She wasn't hungry. Melody yawned, and Howie had to hold his head up with his hand. They sat with the rest of their class in the cafeteria at Rock Castle.

"The next time you want to make up rocky fairy tales by moonlight, count me out," Eddie said, yawning with his mouth full of muffin.

"This isn't a fairy tale," Liza said. "And I'm not making it up. You saw Mrs. Granite talking to that statue the same as I did."

"That means nothing," Eddie snapped. "My grandmother talks to her plants but that doesn't mean she's planning to rob a bank."

Howie nodded. "Eddie has a point. Lots of people talk to things. My dad talks to his computer."

"And my mother talks to pot roasts," Melody added.

Her friends stared at her. "Why does your mom talk to food?" Liza asked.

Melody shrugged. "She's not the best cook and she thinks talking to food will make sure it turns out okay."

"So the only thing we've learned from Liza's late-night adventure is that Melody's mom is a disaster in the kitchen," Eddie grumbled.

"It may not prove anything," Liza said slowly, "but I still think there's something odd about a geologist who talks to statues in the middle of the night."

"The only thing odd is that Mrs. Granite isn't as tired as we are," Howie said, looking across the cafeteria. Mrs. Granite had just hurried into the room, carrying a big box.

"Gather round. We have a busy day planned for you," Mrs. Granite announced. The third-graders hurried to dump their trash and take their trays to the kitchen before clustering around Mrs. Granite. "Today you will be going on a treasure hunt."

Eddie hopped up and down, rubbing his hands together. "Now you're talking," he said. "Point me in the direction of that treasure and let's forget all this talk about rocks."

Mrs. Granite smiled. "The treasure I'm talking about *is* rocks," she told him. She reached in the box and pulled out pads of paper for each student. Next she gave them each a package of colored pencils and a magnifying glass. "The notebook is for you to draw the different types of rocks you find on our hike," she explained. "You can use your magnifying glass to investigate the beauty hidden within each rock."

Eddie flopped down on a nearby chair

and sighed. "A rock is a rock," he mumbled. "A magnifying glass can't change that."

Mrs. Granite shook her head. "Each rock you find at Rock Castle State Park is a unique individual," she said, "made up of tiny particles that have been joined together through time. Every stone is a creation caused by the combined forces of water and wind. Today you have the opportunity to get to know the rocks of my world."

"Did you hear that?" Liza asked her friends as soon as the other third-graders followed Mrs. Granite out of the dining room. "Mrs. Granite believes each rock has a personality."

"She's right," Eddie mumbled. "Rocks have more personality than you."

"Very funny, pebble breath," Liza said. "Go ahead and make jokes now. You won't have time to laugh if Mrs. Granite gets her hands on Mrs. Jeepers' magic brooch."

"We won't have time to catch up with everybody if we stand around here," Howie pointed out. "I don't want to be stranded alone at Rock Castle for the entire day."

Liza shrieked. "This is the last place I'd want to be stranded," she said as she and her friends rushed after the rest of the class.

Their class was already outside and making their way toward a small stone hut behind the castle. The little building was carved out of rock and looked more like a cave than a building. Mrs. Granite knocked on the door. Liza pulled her friends closer to the front of the class so she could hear what Mrs. Granite was telling their teacher.

Mrs. Granite smiled at Mrs. Jeepers. "Today's trail is long and dusty. Perhaps it would be better if you allowed me to lock your beautiful pin safely away."

The four kids held their breath. Mrs. Jeepers never took off her magic brooch.

Mrs. Granite slowly reached for the pin at Mrs. Jeepers' throat. Mrs. Granite's fingers were only inches away when Mrs. Jeepers calmly flashed her eyes. "That is not necessary," their teacher told Mrs. Granite.

"But it would be such a terrible loss if it came loose while you were hiking," Mrs. Granite said kindly. "It looks very valuable."

Mrs. Jeepers nodded. "This stone has been in my family for generations and in my possession for a very long time," she said, her voice carrying a hint of warning. "I shall not part with it now . . . or ever!"

6

Hoodoos

"I told you Mrs. Granite was trying to get her hands on Mrs. Jeepers' brooch," Liza told her friends as they followed the rest of the kids down a sandy trail.

"She was only trying to help," Melody said. "She was afraid Mrs. Jeepers would lose her pin. After all, why would she want Mrs. Jeepers' jewelry?"

"She is a geologist," Howie pointed out. "Maybe she knows the stone is valuable."

Eddie pushed his baseball cap down over his curly red hair. "I hate to admit it, but I think Melody is right. After all, if Mrs. Granite really did want that pin, she would have come with us on this hike and tried to get it from Mrs. Jeepers once we were way out in the middle of nowhere."

Liza admitted that made sense. Mr. Ore, their trail guide, had appeared from the small hut. He was tall, with coal-black hair, black eyes, and dark skin. Thick knobby muscles wrapped around his arms and legs. As soon as Mrs. Granite had introduced him to Mrs. Jeepers and the rest of the third-graders, Mrs. Granite disappeared back into Rock Castle.

"Do you think Mr. Ore lives in that little cave behind Rock Castle?" Howie asked his friends.

"It looks like a cool place to live, if you ask me," Eddie said.

The trail Mr. Ore followed slowly zigzagged its way to the top of the cliff that towered over Rock Castle. Mr. Ore and Mrs. Jeepers led the way. The rest of the kids followed them up the trail. Liza, Melody, Howie, and Eddie stayed at the back of the line.

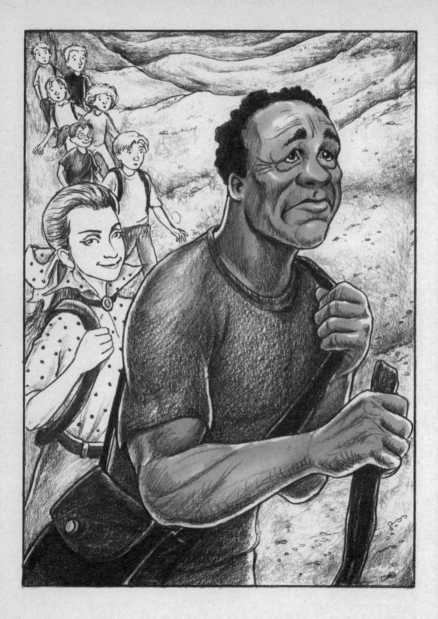

Liza had to breathe hard to keep up. "This path is too steep," she complained.

"I bet Mr. Ore won't have a problem climbing," Melody said. "His muscles look as hard as rock."

But Melody was wrong. Mr. Ore walked slower and slower. Soon he stopped altogether. He drew in a long breath before bending down and picking up a small stone. "This rock," he said in a voice as rough as sand, "is a perfect example of how time changes everything." He passed the rock to a boy named Huey before continuing to speak. "Many people believe a rock is made of a single material. Actually, rocks are made of many things. Time destroys rocks, eroding them down into tiny pieces called sediment."

Mrs. Jeepers nodded. "Those pieces eventually harden together into new rocks called sedimentary rocks," she added.

The kids used their magnifying glasses

to look at the tiny particles in the rock Mr. Ore passed around. Several kids picked up other rocks from the trail and opened their notebooks to sketch them. Eddie opened his notebook, too, but he drew a picture of a saber-toothed tiger getting ready to pounce on Liza.

"You'd better pay attention," Howie warned. "This is important stuff."

Instead of listening to his friend, Eddie drew a picture of Howie about to be munched by a *Tyrannosaurus rex.*

Mr. Ore waited until the kids were finished sketching. Then he started back up the trail. Giant rocks on top of the silent cliffs seemed to watch the kids, and the wind constantly howled around the rocks. The wind made it sound as if the cliffs were moaning. Liza shivered even though the sun was warm on her skin.

The farther they walked, the more Mr. Ore's feet dragged through the dust on the trail. "My feet feel like lead," he mumbled to Mrs. Jeepers. But he said it loud enough that Liza could hear.

Finally, they reached the top of the trail. Mr. Ore pointed to the cliff on the far side of the canyon. "An ancient ocean once covered this land," he explained. "It helped create the cliffs by moving and pressing sediment together. Look closely and you will see the layers of sediment on the cliff face. These cliffs hold the secrets of this land."

Everyone turned to a new page in their

notebooks and began sketching the cliffs. They used different colored pencils to show the lines of minerals and sediments in the rock walls. Everybody, that is, except Eddie. He drew a picture of aliens landing on the cliffs and shooting lasers at his class.

"What made those funny-looking rocks?" a girl named Carey asked.

The kids had all noticed the rock formations lining the tops of the cliffs. Mrs. Jeepers smiled. "I am so glad you have noticed the differences in rock," she said. "Those pinnacles were made by the forces of rain, snow, ice, and wind. As time passed, the rocks eroded or wore away into what you see today."

Mr. Ore waited until Mrs. Jeepers finished. "There are other forces at work as well," he said softly. "At least, that's what the legends tell us."

"What legends?" Eddie hollered. He figured a story was better than the explanation Mrs. Jeepers had given them.

Mr. Ore sighed. "It is not a happy story," he warned the kids.

"That's okay. We don't really like stories with happily-ever-after endings," Eddie told him.

The third-graders gathered near as Mr. Ore spoke. "According to legend, these rocks are called hoodoos, and they aren't rocks at all. Once, an ancient clan of creatures with the power to change their shapes inhabited these very cliffs. They mostly kept to themselves, only leaving the cliffs to hunt. But one day one of the creatures committed a deed so horrible, the entire clan was frozen in time as a punishment."

Carey raised her hand. "Punishing everyone wasn't fair. That's like when we all miss recess because of something Eddie did."

Eddie stuck out his tongue at Carey, but Mr. Ore nodded. "The creatures agreed with you. That is why if you look closely at the faces of these hoodoos it seems as though they are angry. Very angry."

He handed binoculars to the kids and showed them how to focus on the hoodoos lining the cliffs across the canyon. Monster faces snarled at the kids.

Mr. Ore sighed. "Being frozen in time would be terrible," he said. "If only we possessed enough power to free them from their fate."

A boy named Huey raised his hand. "You act as if that story and those rocks are real."

Mr. Ore nodded. "These rocks *are* real," he said, patting a nearby boulder. "They have existed long before us and will be here long after we're gone. If only they could tell us the things they have seen as they stood guard on these cliffs."

Liza used the binoculars to examine the giant pinnacles lining the cliff across from where they stood. That's when she saw something move. She twirled the

knob on top of the binoculars to focus on a person standing near one of the hoo-doos. It was Mrs. Granite, and it looked like the geologist was talking to the hoodoo.

Liza blinked. Was it her imagination, or did one of the hoodoos just move?

7

Pet Rocks

That evening, the kids put on their bathing suits and gathered around a small lake. The lake sat at the base of a cliff lined with silent hoodoos. A waterfall spilled from the cliff right into the lake. Mrs. Jeepers and Mr. Ore sat at a nearby picnic table, sipping tomato juice.

"Aren't you going to go swimming?" Eddie asked Mrs. Jeepers and Mr. Ore in his most polite voice. He was hoping his teacher would jump in. He wanted to splash her.

Mrs. Jeepers shook her head. "I prefer dry, cool places," she said.

"Like a coffin," Melody said under her breath.

"How about you?" Liza asked Mr. Ore. "Are you getting in the water?" Liza

knew a tidal wave would wash over everything if somebody as big as Mr. Ore jumped in. She didn't want to be nearby if that happened.

"I can't swim," Mr. Ore admitted. "I sink like a lump of coal."

"Or like one of those hoodoos," Liza blurted and pointed to the pinnacles high overhead.

Mr. Ore looked deep into Liza's eyes before nodding. "Yes. A rock creature would certainly sink."

Mrs. Jeepers didn't notice Liza's trembles. "Not all rocks sink," Mrs. Jeepers told them. "Pumice made from volcano lava floats in water."

"Well, I plan to do more than float," Eddie interrupted. Before his teacher could start teaching another lesson, he turned and made his way to the side of the lake. Liza, Melody, and Howie hurried after him.

Eddie didn't care about rocks, hoodoos, or anything else. He was too busy planning to splash everybody. He took another step toward the water, but Liza grabbed his arm.

"We can't go swimming yet. We have to talk," she told him. "It's important."

Eddie reluctantly followed his friends to the waterfall. Liza looked around to make sure no one else could hear them over the sound of the water splashing into the lake. She spoke in a voice so low her friends had to lean close to hear.

"I figured out why Mrs. Granite needs Mrs. Jeepers' brooch," she told them. "Mrs. Granite and Mr. Ore are trying to figure out a way to bring these rock monsters to life and they need Mrs. Jeepers' magic brooch to do it."

"You have gone completely crazy," Eddie said. "A rock cannot be brought to life."

"Eddie is right," Howie said. "Maybe you got too much sun today and you're a little confused."

"I am not confused," Liza said. She

stomped her foot to prove her point. When she did, she stepped in a puddle and splattered her friends.

"Calm down," Eddie said. "I'm sure you're not right, but I think it would be neat if rocks could come to life. I'd make friends with one and call him Rocky. Then I'd teach him to stomp on playground bullies."

Melody giggled. "I heard people used to buy pet rocks. If I had one I'd name it Susan."

"Susan is a silly name for a rock," Liza said. "I think Chip is a better name."

"I'd name my rock Buddy Boulder," Howie said, "because I'd have a big one like that."

Howie pointed to a hoodoo right above their heads. The hoodoo's angry face glared back down at them.

"That's probably the kind Mrs. Jeepers would pick, too," Melody added.

Liza gulped. "What if Mrs. Jeepers figures out how to make them come to life?"

she asked. "Maybe that's why she wanted to come to Rock Castle in the first place. She could have rock monsters ready to take over Bailey City."

"We came here to study dumb rocks," Eddie said, "not so our teacher could create an army of rock monsters."

Liza shook her head. "Think about it. There are rocks at the Shelley Museum, which is much closer to Bailey City. But there aren't any huge ones like this at the museum."

"So what?" Melody said.

"Besides," Eddie said, "nobody can make monsters do anything. That's why they're called monsters."

Liza looked over to make sure Mrs. Jeepers couldn't hear. She took a big breath before explaining, "Mrs. Jeepers could use her magic brooch to make monsters do whatever she says."

"I wish she would start by making you close your mouth," Eddie said. "You are wasting all of our swimming time with these silly make-believe stories."

"All you think about is yourself," Liza told Eddie. "I guess it's up to me to get to the bottom of this rock monster mystery."

Eddie laughed. "I'll help you get to the bottom," he said. "The rock bottom."

Then, with one quick motion, Eddie pushed Liza into the lake.

8

Rock Monsters

The sun was barely over the top of the cliffs the next morning when Mrs. Jeepers and Mr. Ore met the kids in front of Rock Castle. "Today we are off on a wonderful adventure," Mr. Ore told the kids. "We are going to find life in rocks!"

Liza choked when she heard his words. "This is it," she whimpered. "We're going on a monster hunt."

"Hush," Howie said. "He's still talking."

"These rocks hold secrets to life millions of years old," Mr. Ore was explaining, "frozen in fossils."

"Fossils?" Liza whimpered.

"See," Melody told her friend. "There are no monsters."

Mr. Ore and Mrs. Jeepers headed down

a new trail. Instead of climbing the cliff like the day before, this trail wound between the rocks on the canyon floor. The trail was sandy and the wind continued to moan from the tops of the cliffs. Liza thought it sounded like hoodoos growling.

The cool wind was so strong it whipped the girls' hair, and Mrs. Jeepers stopped to tuck her long red hair beneath a polka-dotted scarf. The kids zipped up their jackets against the breeze and Mr. Ore rubbed his hands together. "This wind makes me stone cold," he mumbled.

Liza slapped her head. "I've got it," she whispered to her friends. "It all makes sense now."

"The only thing that makes sense is that it's too early in the morning to get blown over the rainbow by this wind," Melody said with a yawn.

Liza shook her head. "This is even worse than I thought," she said.

"Nothing is worse than the things you think up," Eddie teased.

Liza pulled on her friends' arms so they would slow down. Soon, the rest of the kids were far ahead and couldn't hear.

"It's not Mrs. Jeepers who wants to build an army of rock monsters," Liza told them. "It really is Mrs. Granite!"

Howie shook his head. "You're getting carried away by the sight of all these rocks," he told her. "Nobody is planning to build an army out of anything. Especially rocks."

"Rocks would make the perfect army," Liza pointed out. "They're indestructible."

"That's not true," Melody said. "Mr. Ore told us yesterday that water and wind erode rocks into tiny particles."

"Mr. Ore would know," Liza said seriously, "because he *is* a rock."

"Now what are you talking about, boulder brains?" Eddie asked.

Liza pulled her friends close to explain. "I think Mrs. Granite has figured out a way to make these rock monsters come to life," she told them. "And Mr. Ore is living, walking, breathing proof."

"Exactly how do you think a nice geologist like Mrs. Granite could make rocks move?" Melody asked.

Liza reminded them of their first night in the castle museum. "Remember when she told us that some people believe gems have powers?"

Melody nodded. "That's not news to us. After all, Mrs. Jeepers has a magic stone in her brooch."

"You figured it out, too!" Liza shrieked.

"Figured out what?" Howie asked.

"That green stone in Mrs. Granite's glass case must be a twin of the gem in Mrs. Jeepers' brooch," Liza explained. "And it has the same kind of magic. Mrs. Granite has learned how to use the gem's magic to bring these rock monsters to life."

"If that were true," Howie said, "then why hasn't she brought them all to life already?"

"Because," Liza said slowly, "one stone isn't powerful enough. That's why she has to get her hands on Mrs. Jeepers' brooch."

Eddie grinned. "I hope Mrs. Granite does get that pin," he said. "Then I can do whatever I want."

"If Mrs. Granite puts the two stones together, all those hoodoos could come to life and we'd be crushed into sand. We have to save Mrs. Jeepers' brooch — even if it means we're doomed to being well-behaved and polite for the rest of our lives!"

9

Lost

Liza, Melody, Eddie, and Howie had to hurry along the trail to catch up with the rest of the kids. Mr. Ore led them deep into the canyon, around sandstone cliffs jutting up from the ground. The sandy trail turned to smooth rock that was easy to walk across. They hiked across a huge rock and climbed down into an old, dried-up creek bed.

Mr. Ore stopped and waited for everyone to gather around him. "Millions of years ago, sea animals lived in this area. As they died they sank to the bottom of the ancient seas that once covered this land. Some became buried in mud. As the oceans got smaller and the land dried, the mud became rock. Next came dinosaurs. They thundered across the land, living and dying where the ocean once was. Like the sea animals, their skeletons became stuck in mud that later turned to rock. Those fossils tell the secret of lives long gone," he told them. "Fossils are sometimes hidden in the very rocks beneath our feet."

"Cool!" Eddie yelled. "I want to find a dinosaur skeleton. Maybe I'm stepping on top of a *Stegosaurus* right now."

Mr. Ore smiled. "Anything is possible. Kids have found dinosaur bones before."

"That's right," Howie agreed. "I read a book about a girl who found a *Tyrannosaurus rex* skeleton."

"Awesome," Eddie said. "Let's look right now."

Mr. Ore and Mrs. Jeepers showed the kids how to slowly brush away the sand with a paintbrush to look for fossils. "Be very careful," Mr. Ore said. "It would be tragic to hurt a rare fossil, for then we would never know the story it has to tell."

Liza groaned. "See," she whispered. "Mr. Ore is helping Mrs. Granite bring all the rocks and fossils back to life."

Howie shook his head. "I think he means that if you destroy the fossil you won't be able to examine it and figure out what animals lived here," he explained.

"I hope you're right," Liza said softly as she glanced up at the cliff walls. Hoodoos stared down at the kids. "Because if you're wrong, we'll be trapped in this canyon with no way out."

"Howie is right," Melody said. "Fossil hunting will be perfectly safe."

"Who cares about fossils? I want to find a *T-rex* skeleton," Eddie told them.

The kids wandered around the creek bed, searching for fossils and dinosaur bones. Melody was the first one to find a fossil of a leaf. After lunch Howie found a rock showing the outline of a small bone. Eddie didn't find anything except clumps of dirt and rocks.

"There are too many people looking here," he told his friends. "There's bound to be better hunting if we follow the creek bed a little bit."

He led his three friends around a boulder. They kept moving, searching for odd shapes embedded in rocks. "This is a waste of time," Eddie finally complained as the kids took a break on a big rock. "There aren't any fossils or bones around here."

"I just hope we don't find a snake by mistake," Melody said.

"A snake!" Liza squealed. "Are there snakes around here?"

"Probably," Howie said. "Snakes like to hide under rocks and crawl into warm places."

"Like sleeping bags," Eddie added.

Liza jumped away from the rock. Eddie stood on the rock and pretended to be a hunter. "Snakes, dinosaurs, and monsters, come out wherever you are."

Liza put her hands on her hips. "That is not funny."

Melody stood up beside Liza. "I think we walked a long way from the other kids," Melody said. Howie, Melody, Eddie, and Liza looked around. There wasn't another kid in sight. The sun was over the cliff wall and long shadows crept across the canyon.

"We're lost!" Liza whimpered. "And it's getting dark! We'll be stranded for the night. What if the rock monsters come alive and grind us into powder?"

"First of all," Eddie said, "there are no rock monsters. Second, we're not lost."

"That's right," Howie said. "We've been following this old creek bed the entire afternoon. All we have to do is follow it back to where we were."

"We'd better head back right away," Melody said. "We've been gone a long time. Mrs. Jeepers will be worried."

"Not to mention mad," Liza said. None of them liked the idea of a vampire teacher being angry with them. The four kids hurried back the way they had come. They hadn't gone far when something stopped them dead in their tracks.

"It's a monster!" Liza screamed.

10

Monster Fossil

The kids stared up at the face of a huge rock wall. There, stuck in the rock, was a giant monster, complete with five arms, two heads, and three legs. "This is better than a dinosaur," Eddie said with a grin.

Liza grabbed Melody by the arm. "I don't want to get eaten by a rock monster."

"That can't be real," Howie said, stepping closer to the monster.

"Don't go near it!" Liza warned.

"It can't hurt me," Howie told her. "It's frozen in rock like a fossil."

"It's a monster fossil," Eddie said. He danced around singing, "Snakes, dinosaurs, and monsters — oh my! Snakes, dinosaurs, and monsters — oh my!"

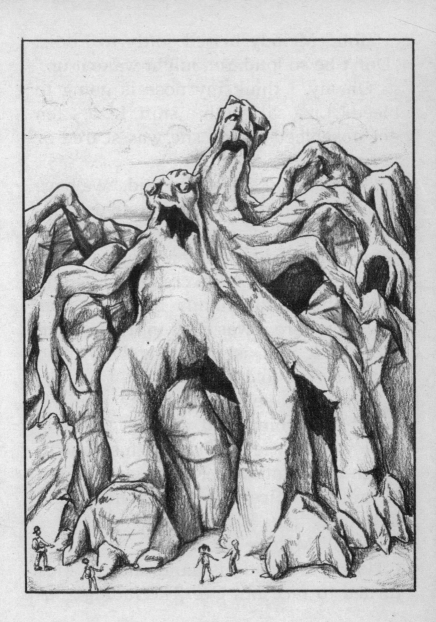

"Shh," Melody hissed softly to Eddie. "Don't be so loud. You might wake it up."

"Oh my, I think my nose is going to bleed," Liza said with a sniff. Liza often got nosebleeds when she was scared or nervous.

"No, you don't," Melody said. "We have enough to worry about without you dripping blood all over the place."

Liza pinched her nose and stared with wide eyes at the huge creature looming before her. She couldn't believe it was real, but there it was right in front of her.

"I think it's just a strangely formed rock," Howie told his friends.

"I've never seen a rock like that before," Liza whimpered.

Slowly, Howie reached out his hand to touch the giant foot of the rock monster. A gravelly voice stopped Howie's hand in midair.

"Stop!" Mr. Ore boomed.

Howie dropped his hand and the kids turned to face Mr. Ore. The fading sunlight shone behind him, making his muscles look even bigger. His gray sweatshirt and pants were the same shade as the rocks around him and his face was a mask of anger. To Liza, Mr. Ore looked like an enraged hoodoo come to life.

"I've been looking all over for you," Mr. Ore told them. "I was afraid you were hurt or lost."

"We were lost," Liza admitted.

"No, we weren't," Eddie said. "I knew where we were the whole time."

Mr. Ore folded his huge arms over his bulging chest. "You were supposed to stay with the group."

"Sorry about that," Melody apologized. "We thought we could find better fossils if we got away from everyone else."

"Look what we found," Eddie said, pointing to the giant fossil.

Mr. Ore stepped back and stared at the huge form in the rock wall. "How did you kids find this?" he asked.

"It was just here," Melody explained.

"It's — it's a monster," Liza stammered. "A rock monster."

Mr. Ore stepped closer to the figure and rubbed his eyes. "It's getting late," he said finally. "Our eyes must be playing tricks on us. Now, follow me back to the others and don't wander off again." Mr. Ore frowned at the kids. "If you do, you'll be sorry. Very sorry."

Liza gulped and walked with her friends behind Mr. Ore. Liza looked over her shoulder and was relieved to see the rock monster hadn't moved. Surely they would be safe when they joined the rest of the kids. A rock monster couldn't eat a whole class of third-graders, could it?

Melody giggled nervously. "I guess it was silly to think that rock monster could be real."

"Oh, it's real," Eddie joked. Then, lowering his voice so Mr. Ore couldn't hear, he said, "That's probably Mr. Ore's long-lost brother. His name is Fred Ore the Bore."

"Very funny," Liza snapped.

"Don't worry." Howie patted Liza on the shoulder. "I'm sure Mr. Ore is right. We're all tired and it is getting dark. Our eyes were playing tricks on us."

"No creature like that ever lived in this world," Melody added.

"I hope you're right," Liza said softly. "Because if you're not, and Mrs. Granite gets her hands on Mrs. Jeepers' brooch, there's no telling what could happen. She might make that rock monster back there come to life and we'll all be in big trouble. Monster trouble!"

11

Missing Magic

"All that hiking wore me out," Liza told her friends when they got back to the cafeteria for dinner.

"I'm glad to be inside, away from the hoodoos. I wish we didn't have to sleep outside," she admitted.

"Who cares?" Eddie said. "At least we get to miss school one more day. I'm starving. Let's eat."

Melody put her head down on the wooden table. "I'm too pooped to eat."

"Not me," Eddie said, irritated that they had to wait for two other tables before they could go through the food line. "I could eat a horse."

"How about a dinosaur?" Howie asked.

Eddie grinned and banged the table. "Bring me one *T-rex* steak, please."

"Oh my gosh," Liza said. "Look at that!"

The kids turned to stare at their teacher as she chatted with Mrs. Granite and Mr. Ore. Mrs. Jeepers had her hand on Mr. Ore's huge muscular arm.

"I think Mrs. Jeepers likes Mr. Ore," Melody said with a giggle.

"Look," Liza said, pointing to their teacher. "Mrs. Jeepers' brooch is missing."

Melody gasped. "That can't be true. She always wears her brooch."

"That's right," Howie said with a gulp. "She said she'd never take it off."

"Maybe she didn't have a choice," Liza told her friends. "Maybe Mrs. Granite and Mr. Ore made her take it off."

"She doesn't look upset to me," Howie said. The kids stared at their teacher. They had never seen her happier. She was laughing and talking. In fact, she was having so much fun she hardly even glanced at the kids.

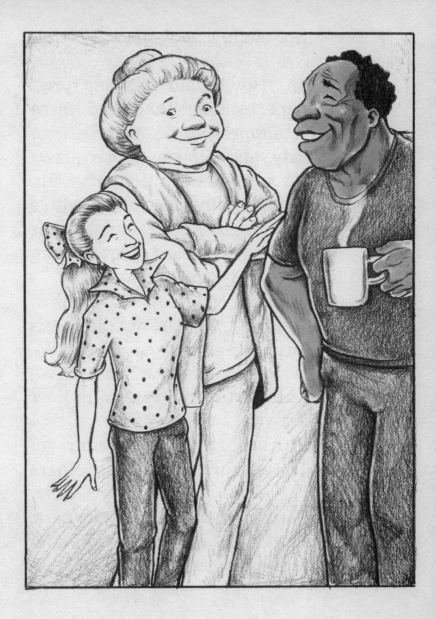

"She's not acting like herself," Liza said.

"Come on," Howie said. "It's our turn." The kids got in line. They had three choices for supper: pizza, spaghetti, or liver. Melody and Howie chose pizza, while Eddie and Liza got the spaghetti.

Carey was the only one in the whole third grade to get liver. Carey patted her curly blond hair. "I heard liver is very good for your hair," she explained.

When they got back to their table, Eddie put a long spaghetti noodle in his red hair and pretended to be Carey. "Doesn't my hair look great?" he asked. "I eat liver all the time. I even drink liver milk shakes."

Liza had to giggle. "You'd better get that out of your hair before Mrs. Jeepers sees."

Eddie glanced over at Mrs. Jeepers. She was batting her eyes at Mr. Ore and smiling. Eddie grinned. "Mrs. Jeepers is busy. It looks like it's time to liven up this rocky class trip."

"What are you going to do?" Howie asked.

Eddie didn't answer, he just stuck a long noodle in his mouth and blew. The noodle blew up and down before finally landing on Eddie's freckled nose. "It's a monster tongue." Melody laughed.

"I can make monster bubbles, too," Eddie said. He put a straw into his chocolate milk carton and blew. Bubbles popped out the top of the carton and oozed over the side. Before long, most of the kids in the cafeteria were blowing bubbles, but Mrs. Jeepers still continued talking to Mr. Ore.

"It looks more like monster snot to me," Howie said, before taking a bite of pizza.

"No, here's monster snot," Eddie said with a laugh. He stuck a pea in the end of his straw.

"Eddie, don't you dare!" Liza warned, but Eddie was too excited to stop. He raised the straw to his lips and blew. The pea splattered right onto Carey's pink shirt.

"Monster snot — direct hit!" Eddie cheered.

Liza frowned at Eddie. "How would you like someone to do that to you?" she asked.

"Don't be such a goody-goody," Eddie said. "Mrs. Jeepers doesn't care."

It was true. Mrs. Jeepers didn't even look at the kids. "Maybe that brooch had all her power," Melody said, "and she's helpless without it."

"My first-grade teacher was mean and she didn't even have a brooch," Howie told his friends.

"Something is very wrong," Liza said. "I'm going to find out what happened to Mrs. Jeeper's brooch if it's the last thing I do."

12

Tower of Doom

That night Liza tossed and turned in her sleeping bag. First she worried a snake would crawl in her tent. Then she worried about Mrs. Jeepers' brooch. What if Mrs. Granite really did have it? Liza was so upset she took a long time getting to sleep. When she finally did nod off she dreamed that Bailey Elementary was filled with rock monsters. All the teachers and even the principal were monsters. For lunch the only thing on the menu was stewed pebbles. Then she looked down and her feet were turning into rocks.

Liza sat upright and woke herself up. She was still at Rock Castle Park in one of the girls' tents. She had to feel her feet just to make sure they weren't rocks.

Liza looked around the tent in the moonlight. Melody and the two other girls were sound asleep. Liza leaned over to Melody. "Melody," Liza whispered. "Wake up."

"What's wrong?" Melody jerked awake.

"I had a bad nightmare," Liza explained. "I can't get back to sleep."

Melody sighed and threw her sleeping bag off. "Maybe some warm milk will help. Let's see if we can find the kitchen."

Liza and Melody tiptoed out of the tent and into an unlocked Rock Castle door. The doorway was well lit so the kids could use the nearby bathroom. "Do you hear that?" Liza whispered.

Melody nodded. It sounded like something was being dragged down the hallway and was coming right for them.

"It's the rock monsters coming to get us," Liza hissed.

"Not if I can help it," Melody said, quickly pulling open a hallway door. It was a storage closet for cleaning products. The girls squeezed inside, but left the door open just a crack so they could peek out.

Two huge shadows slowly came down the hall. Liza and Melody held their breath as the shadows got closer and closer. Liza felt like she was going to faint. She didn't want to be a monster's midnight snack.

Melody was relieved to see that the two shadows belonged to none other than Howie and Eddie. As the boys passed the closet Melody jumped out behind them.

"Arrgh!" Howie shouted and jumped into Eddie. Eddie fell to the floor and covered his face.

Liza hopped out of the closet and giggled. "We scared Eddie."

Eddie scrambled to his feet. "I'm not afraid of anything," he said. "Especially girls. Howie made me fall down."

"We're just looking for something to eat," Howie explained.

Melody pointed down the hall. "We're heading to the kitchen, too. I think it's this way."

"Maybe I can check out what's behind that mysterious locked door in the rock museum," Eddie said.

Liza shook her head. "Mrs. Granite said it was just a storage room."

"Maybe it's for hoodoo storage," Eddie said.

Liza shivered at the thought of strange creatures being kept in a big hidden closet. She was sure she didn't want to go in a room like that.

The kids paused at the door to the rock museum. "Do we have to go this way?" Liza whimpered.

Melody nodded. "It's the only way."

Liza held her breath as the kids made their way through the tables of rocks. It was nearly pitch-black in the room. The only light came from a few of the wall displays that were lit with an eerie yellow glow. "Oh no," Liza squealed. "The green stone from the case is missing!"

Sure enough, there was an empty spot where the green stone had been. "It's true," Liza told her friends. "Mrs. Granite has both green stones. She's going to use them to bring the rock monsters to life."

Melody started to argue, but a strange noise stopped her. It sounded like it was coming from behind the very same locked door Eddie had tried to open when they first came to Rock Castle.

"Something is in there," Eddie said firmly, "and there's only one way to find out what it is."

"No!" Liza said, but Eddie tried the doorknob anyway. This time, the door creaked open to reveal a spiral staircase leading up and up and up.

"You have to go first," Melody told Eddie.

"Why me?" Eddie said.

Liza put her hands on her hips. "You just said you weren't afraid of anything. This is your chance to prove it."

Eddie gulped and slowly headed up the steps with his friends following closely behind. They wound round and round. The only light came from the moonlight shining through a tiny window at the top of the twisting staircase. Wind whistled and howled through the window and down the steps, scattering goose bumps over their arms.

"I don't like this," Howie said. "It reminds me of a scary movie I once saw called *The Tower of Doom*."

"Were there statues in that movie?" Eddie asked when he reached the top.

Howie shook his head. "No."

"Well, there are here," Eddie said as the kids came into a small tower room filled with marble statues.

"This is strange," Melody whispered.

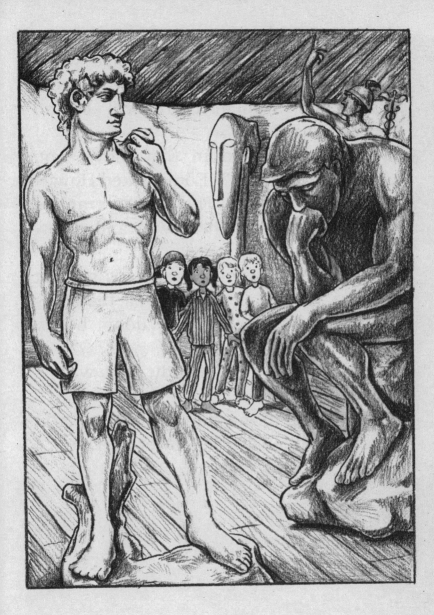

"I bet this is where Mrs. Granite brings her rock monsters to life," Liza whispered. "And now that she has Mrs. Jeepers' magic brooch, there will be no stopping her."

"What happened in that movie you were talking about?" Eddie asked Howie.

Howie shrugged. "The bad guy trapped the good guys in the tower and threw away the key."

Liza shivered and said, "Let's get out of here." She had one foot on the steps going down when the door below slammed shut.

"We're too late," Melody said with a gasp.

Liza clung to the stair railing in terror. "We're trapped in the Tower of Doom!"

13

Monster Battle

"Someone trapped us in here," Liza squealed.

Howie pointed to the small open window above the stairs. "Maybe the wind caused the door to slam shut."

"I bet that's what happened," Melody said.

"But we're still trapped up here with these monsters," Liza said, pointing to the statues that filled the tower.

Eddie grunted and slapped one of the statues on the shoulder. "These aren't even good monsters."

"Eddie's right," Howie said as he examined the statues for the first time. "These look more like sculptures from an art museum than monsters."

Liza and Melody looked closely at the

statues. They were carved out of marble and polished so that they almost glowed. "Somebody sure knows how to bring this marble to life," Melody said with amazement. "They look almost real."

Liza sat on the top step with a grunt. "I really wish you hadn't said that," she muttered.

Suddenly Liza jumped up and pointed to the door below. "Someone is down there," she whispered. Her three friends huddled beside her to listen.

Scratch. Scratch. Scratch.

"The rock monsters are coming to get us," Liza whispered. "They're probably going to bring these creatures to life, too."

"They won't get me without a fight," Eddie snapped.

All four kids dug in their pockets for weapons. Melody pulled a wad of fuzz out of her pocket. Howie had his magnifying glass in his pj's pocket. Liza had no

pockets, but Eddie had a pad and pencil in his shorts' pocket. "Great," Eddie complained. "All I can do is draw the monsters before they pound me into pebbles."

Squeak!

Liza closed her eyes as the door swung slowly open. "Is it a monster?" she asked.

Eddie nodded. "The worst kind."

"Very funny," Melody said. "It's Mrs. Jeepers."

"I've never been so glad to see a vampire in my life," Howie whispered.

Mrs. Jeepers stomped up the steps. Mrs. Granite and Mr. Ore were right behind her.

As Mrs. Jeepers stepped into the tower, Melody tapped Liza on the shoulder. "Mrs. Jeepers is wearing her brooch," Melody whispered.

"We've been looking for you," Mrs. Jeepers said with a frown.

"We . . . we found these," Liza said, pointing to the statues.

"I see you've discovered my sculptures," said Mrs. Granite.

"That's right," Liza said boldly. "And we know all about them."

Mrs. Granite smiled. "My secret surprise is out, then. I was going to show you these tomorrow. I do enjoy making life from cold stone."

"So you admit you made these?" Melody asked.

Mr. Ore nodded. "Mrs. Granite is a wonderful artist."

"Artist?" Eddie asked.

"I find beauty buried in the marble," Mrs. Granite said.

"But what about your brooch?" Liza asked Mrs. Jeepers. "We thought Mrs. Granite took it."

"That's right," Howie said. "You weren't acting like yourself. We thought something was wrong."

"How kind of you to be concerned," Mrs. Jeepers said. "I decided Mrs. Granite was right, so I pinned the brooch in-

side my shirt pocket for safekeeping."

Eddie reached out to pull Liza's pigtail. "See," Eddie told Liza, "you had nothing to worry about."

Mrs. Jeepers flashed her eyes at Eddie and rubbed her brooch. Eddie sighed and put his hands in his pockets. "Everything is back to normal now," Mrs. Jeepers said with her odd little half smile.

Mrs. Granite led the group down the steps. Eddie and Howie were the last ones down.

Eddie frowned and whispered to his friend, "With Mrs. Jeepers as our teacher, nothing at Bailey Elementary will ever be normal!"

Monster
Activities
and Puzzles

Monster Maze

The Bailey School kids are lost. Can you help them find the trail that leads back to their campsite?

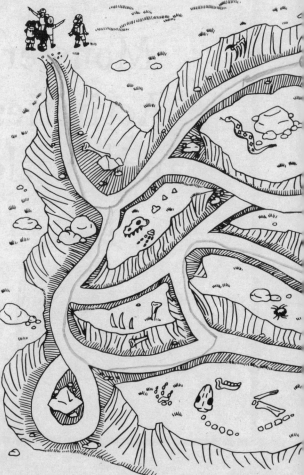

Answer on page 119

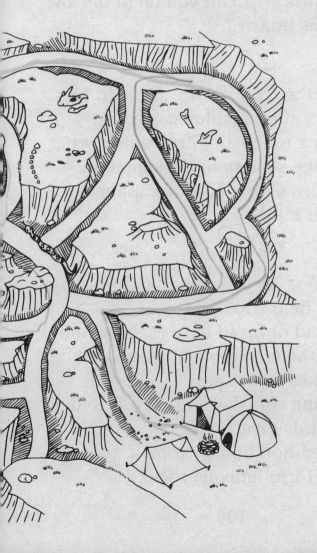

Campfire Crossword

Now that you've read *Mrs. Jeepers' Monster Class Trip,* can you fill in the answers to this puzzle?

Down
1. What is the color of the stone in Mrs. Granite's glass display case?
4. According to the kids' trail guide, what reveals the secrets of lives gone by?
7. What does Carey eat for supper after the fossil hunt?

Across
2. What does Mrs. Jeepers' class study on their field trip?
3. What kind of fossil does Melody find?
5. What is the last name of the man who leads hikes at the park?
6. The name of the park the Bailey School kids visit is Rock _____.
8. What red-hot liquid from a volcano cools to form igneous rock?

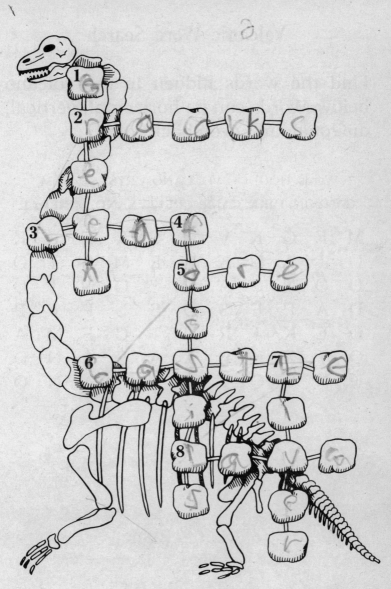

Answer on page 119

Volcanic Word Search

Find the words hidden in the volcano below. Words can be horizontal, vertical, diagonal, and even backward!

Words: HOODOO, VOLCANO, CRYSTAL, GEM, CANYON, HIKE, CAMP, CREEK, SAND, MINERAL

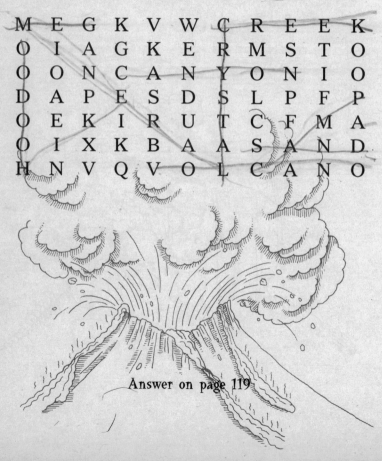

```
M E G K V W C R E E K
O I A G K E R M S T O
O O N C A N Y O N I O
D A P E S D S L P F P
O E K I R U T C F M A
O I X K B A A S A N D
H N V Q V O L C A N O
```

Answer on page 119

Crystal Pops

You may need a grown-up to help you with this recipe.

Ice cube tray
Fruit juice
Plastic wrap
Popsicle sticks

Fill an ice cube tray with fruit juice. Wrap a sheet of plastic wrap around the top of the tray. Poke one Popsicle stick through the plastic wrap into each cube. The plastic wrap will help the stick stand up straight until the juice freezes. Place the tray in the freezer until the juice is solid. Remove from the freezer. Take off the plastic wrap and get ready to rock!

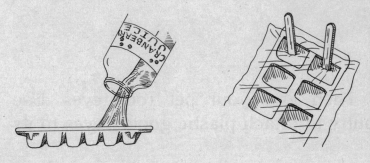

Make Your Own Pet Rock

You will need:
Scissors
Construction paper
A rock the size of
    your fist
Poster putty or
    craft glue
Markers

Optional:
Plastic googly eyes
Pipe cleaners
Yarn
Stickers
Glitter

Here's a fun way to bring rocks to life:
Use the scissors to cut two feet out of construction paper. The feet can be any shape and size you'd like — but ovals work nicely. Attach each foot to the bottom of your rock using a piece of poster putty the size of a dime.

Then give your pet rock eyes. Use putty to attach plastic googly eyes to its face — or draw eyes on the surface with a fun marker, gel pen, or glitter pen.

You can give your pet rock antennae or even arms by attaching pipe cleaners to the top of its head or the sides of its body.

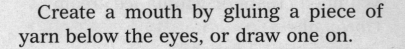

Create a mouth by gluing a piece of yarn below the eyes, or draw one on.

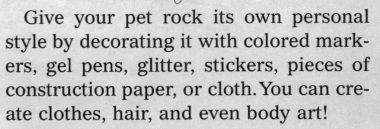

Give your pet rock its own personal style by decorating it with colored markers, gel pens, glitter, stickers, pieces of construction paper, or cloth. You can create clothes, hair, and even body art!

Don't forget to name your new pet!

Sediment Mud Pie

You may need a grown-up to help you with this recipe.

A box of instant chocolate pudding mix (plus the ingredients listed on the box)
About 16–20 of your favorite cookies (chocolate chip or graham crackers work well)
A box of animal crackers
Whipped cream or vanilla ice cream
Optional:
Pieces of dried fruit
Gummy candy

Follow the directions on the box to make the chocolate pudding. Let the pudding set in the refrigerator for about half an hour. Meanwhile, place your favorite cookies in a large resealable plastic bag. Crush them into coarse crumbs using the back of a spoon. If you like, you can add some pieces of dried fruit to the cookie-crumb mixture. Then cover the bottom of 4 small drinking glasses (or a medium-size clear bowl) with half of the cookie crumbs. This is the bottom layer of sedimentary rock.

Next, spoon half the chocolate pudding on top of the "sediment." Sprinkle animal crackers and more cookie crumbs on top of the pudding. If you like, you can add some gummy bears or other animal-shaped candy. Then add the rest of the pudding over the animals. Now you have "fossils" of woolly mammoths and saber-toothed tigers buried in muddy sediment!

Then top it off with a "snowy" scoop of whipped cream or vanilla ice cream. Grab a spoon and get ready to dig for fossils!

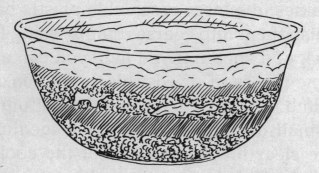

Have Your Own Fossil Hunt

Want to go on your own fossil hunt? Here's a great game to play with a group of friends. You can play it in your backyard, in your house, or even on the playground. Just have one person hide up to fifteen "fossils." The fossils may be feathers, seashells, rocks, cards, or pencils. Then let the hunt begin! The person who finds the most fossils in fifteen minutes wins!

Hint: If you have an adult hide the fossils, everyone gets to play.

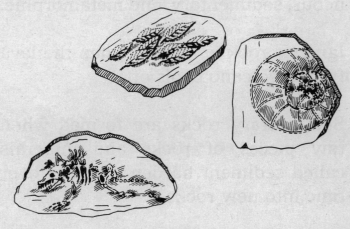

Rock-solid Facts

A geologist is a scientist who studies the history of the earth through rocks. Are you a geologist-in-training? How many of these rock-solid facts did you catch as you read *Mrs. Jeepers' Monster Class Trip*?

- Painite is a type of crystal. It is priceless because there are only three known pieces of painite crystal in existence — and nobody knows where those are!

- There are three main types of rock: igneous, sedimentary, and metamorphic.

- Igneous rock is formed when the lava from a volcano cools off.

- Sedimentary rocks are formed when tiny pieces of rocks and minerals called sediment harden together over time into new rocks.

- Extinct volcanoes will probably never erupt again.

- Dormant volcanoes are sleeping. They haven't erupted for a long time, but they still might.

- Active volcanoes may erupt at any time.

- Some cliffs were made by ancient oceans. The strong ocean currents moved and pressed sediment (particles of rocks and minerals) together. If you look closely, you can see layers of sediment and minerals on the faces of some cliffs.

- The forces of rain, snow, ice, and wind all erode or wear away rock over time, creating rounded edges and even interesting shapes like hoodoos.

- Pumice is a type of rock made from volcano lava. It floats in water.

- Fossils were formed when the remains of plants and animals (like leaves and bones) became buried in mud. As the land dried, the mud hardened into rock — and the fossils became stuck in the rocks! Most of what scientists know about dinosaurs comes from studying their fossils.

Puzzle Answers

Monster Maze

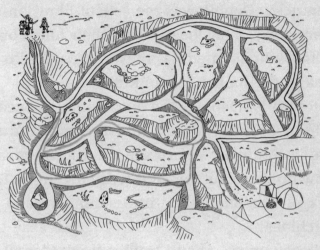

Campfire Crossword

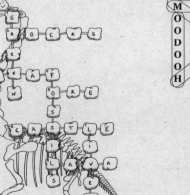

Volcanic Word Search

M	E	G	K	V	W	C	R	E	E	K
O	I	A	G	K	E	R	M	S	T	O
O	O	N	C	A	N	Y	O	N	I	O
D	A	P	E	S	D	S	L	P	F	P
O	E	K	I	R	U	T	C	F	M	A
I	X	K	B	A	A	S	A	N	D
H	N	V	Q	V	O	L	C	A	N	O

119

Debbie Dadey and Marcia Thornton Jones have fun writing stories together. When they both worked at an elementary school in Lexington, Kentucky, Debbie was the school librarian and Marcia was a teacher. During their lunch break in the school cafeteria, they came up with the idea of the Bailey School kids.

Recently Debbie and her family moved to Aurora, Illinois. Marcia and her husband still live in Kentucky where she continues to teach. How do these authors still write together? They talk on the phone and use computers and fax machines!

Learn more about Debbie and Marcia on their Web site, www.BaileyKids.com!